Goodnight Golda

A handbook for brave Jewish girls and their mighty friends

CW01551226

By Batya Bricker

With Ilana Stein

Batya Bricker

Published by Batya Bricker
Batya Bricker Book Projects
PO Box 28819, Sandringham, Johannesburg, 2192
batya@batyabricker.co.za

Copyright © 2021 Batya Bricker

Cover Design and layout: Mary-Anne van der Byl
Illustration: Mary-Anne van der Byl and Ronel Pienaar

Printed and bound by Novus Print, a division of Novus Holdings.

ISBN number: 978-0-620-92781-9

All rights reserved.
No part of this book may be reproduced or transmitted in any form or by any electronic or mechanical means, including photocopying and recording, or by any other information storage or retrieval system, without written permission from the publisher.

Part of the proceeds from this book will be donated to women and girl beneficiaries identified by The Angel Network in South Africa, an organization founded by a group of amazing Jewish women, who work tirelessly to alleviate poverty and empower communities to reach their full potential. For more information, please visit theangelnetwork.co.za.

This book belongs to:

_____

Your only limit is you.
Be brave.
Be fearless.
Be you!

Dedication

Behind every successful woman is herself.*

*with a little help from a cheerleading crew.

To the head cheerleader of mine, Rafi. you make everything possible. Thank you.

Batya

What does being brave look like?

Dear reader,

Fearlessness can be many things – it can mean working to save others from suffering, speaking up against wrong, it can be saving lives or inspiring a new way of thinking. It can be swimming against the stream and daring to do what no (wo) man has done before.

In these pages, you will find all kinds of different of ladies with pluck – from fashionista Donna Karan to the freedom fighter Helen Suzman, business mogul Dona Gracia Nasi to educator Sarah Schnenirer, and of course Golda Meir, from whom this book gets its title. They come from all across the globe – Hungary, Israel, South Africa, USA, Ethiopia, the UK, Canada and India – and reach out to us across the ages, from biblical times to today.

All these women searched for and found something special only they could give to the world. It probably wasn't easy, or comfortable, or without heartache. But they did it anyway. And the world is forever changed.

With this book, I invite you to explore what bravery looks like to you, and to bring it into your life.

There's a Jewish teaching that says that "bishvili nivrah haolam" – for me, the world was created.

Who you are, the family you were born to, the strengths you have, the weaknesses you have, the friends you have, the friends you don't have, whether you're beautiful, or brainy, or talented, or none of those things – absolutely everything in your life is there for a reason – to help you grow, to reach your highest potential, to be your best self, and make your unique contribution to the world.

Its up to you to find those reasons.

The world is waiting for you. Step into your light.

With all my blessings and love,
Batya

Ladies with pluck

Ladies with pluck

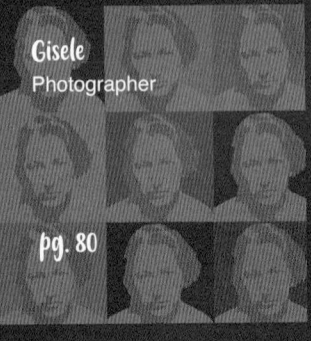
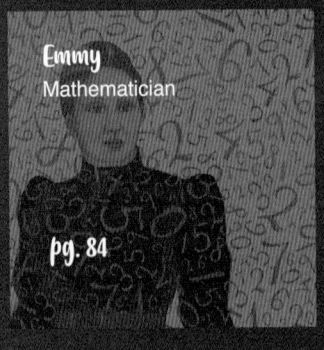
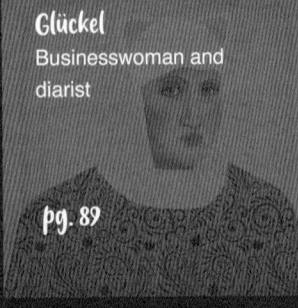

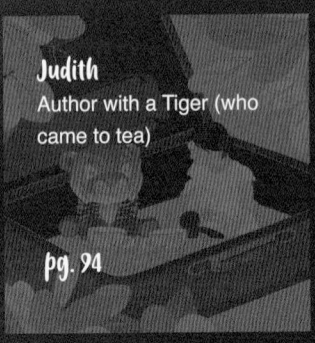

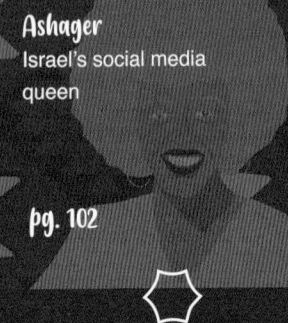

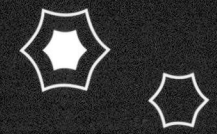

"Your greatness is not what you have,
it's what you give."

Golda

Golda Meir
Israeli Prime Minister and "Iron Bobba"
Poland, United States, Israel
1898 – 1978

What makes a home?

The answer to this question was something Golda Meir would fight for her whole life.

Golda was 14 when she ran away from hers. Her parents wanted her to marry young, to have children and act like a pretty lady. They didn't want her to be educated, or to be outspoken, or to make grand changes in the world. But Golda didn't fit the mould. She did not care for things like makeup and lipstick and how she looked. She knew she had a special talent – the gift of words – and she wanted to use it for more important things.

Like books. Once, when many of her classmates did not have school books, she tried raising money, but without much luck. Bravely, she convinced the owner of a theatre to allow her to use the venue for one night. She and her friends did not know any actors, nor did they have a play prepared, but Golda had a plan. She went out on to that empty stage all alone, with nothing but the butterflies in her stomach for company. When it was time to start, Golda walked up to the microphone ... and the audience was hooked. The star of the show was Golda, and her speech was all it took to raise enough money to buy books for her school.

Golda loved teaching, but her passion for helping her fellow Jews was stronger. After she married, Golda travelled across the world to make a home on a kibbutz in Israel. There, Golda found her superpower was needed more than ever.

The Holocaust had just ended, and the world needed to hear what the Jewish people had lost. They needed to hear that the Jewish people wanted to make a safe haven in Israel. That it was time for the Jewish people to come home.

Golda would travel the world using her voice to melt the hearts of politicians and kings. One night in Chicago, Golda, standing all alone on a brightly lit stage, faced an audience of thousands, and using only the power of her voice convinced the audience to donate $50 million to help set up a permanent Jewish state.

"When the history of Israel is written," stated Israel's first prime minister, David Ben-Gurion, "it will say that there was a Jewish woman who got the money to make the State possible."

Because of her special power, Golda was the only woman present when the historic Declaration of Independence of the State of Israel was signed. She went on to become the first and (so far) only female Prime Minister of Israel, the brand new home of the Jewish people.

"Trust yourself. Create the kind of self that you will be happy to live with all your life."

Golda Meir

Vera

Vera Cooper Rubin
Astrophysicist and stargirl
USA
1926 – 2016

Always follow your north star, no matter what others may say.

Vera was 10 years old when she fell in love with the night sky.

She would climb onto the roof of her parents' house to watch the stars while her family slept. When she was 14, she built herself a homemade telescope out of cardboard to watch the meteors as they streaked across the inky heavens. She wanted to study the stars more than anything, and was delighted when she received a place at Vassar, an all-girls university, to study astronomy.

What she really wanted to do was study at Princeton, but back then girls were not allowed in.
In fact, for much of her life, she struggled to be taken seriously – since when do women become astronomers, they said?

Later when she worked at the Palomar Observatory, there wasn't even a women's bathroom, as no women had ever worked there! But she wasn't put off, she just made her own bathroom and became the first female astronomer to watch the skies there.

Vera was on her way to becoming a famous astrophysicist, which is a scientist that studies the life cycles of the stars, planets and other things that whirl through space. She was the first to realise how galaxies clumped together rather than

spread, a fact that her male counterparts would only discover 20 years later.

People think that space is generally an empty vacuum, dimpled with starlight. But it was Vera who noticed that stars orbiting the outer rims of galaxies were going at extremely high speeds – which means that there is a lot of mass around which they must circle. That mass or matter is invisible – and most of the universe, we now know, is made up of it. It's called dark matter and Vera was the one who confirmed what it was that we could not see.

She may have started with a cardboard telescope, but in 2019, a state-of-the-art telescope was named after her: the Vera C. Rubin Observatory in Chile. Vera had become a guiding star for all other women reaching for theirs.

"In my own life, my science and my religion are separate. I'm Jewish, and so religion to me is a kind of moral code and a kind of history. I try to do my science in a moral way, and, I believe that, ideally, science should be looked upon as something that helps us understand our role in the universe."

Vera Cooper Rubin

Bertha

"Only a girl". That's probably what baby Bertha would have heard on the day of her birth.

Born in Vienna in 1859 to a middle-class, wealthy, religious family, Bertha always knew that her parents would have preferred a son. For a girl in Bertha's social class, her future only showed her becoming a lady of leisure, waiting for the ideal husband, perhaps doing some charity work, a bit of reading, and of course, embroidery. Ooh, exciting! Not.

For Bertha that just looked boring.

Bertha wanted to make a difference, to women and girls especially. Yes, she was happy to help in soup kitchens and do social work, but she wanted to help women to be educated, and be given rights, just like men.

So Bertha created and ran the *Judischer Frauenbund* (League of Jewish Women) where she aimed to educate girls. She helped with in-job training so that they could stand on their own two (albeit dainty) feet. She established a national network of Jewish social workers to help protect women. She created an orphanage and home for unwed mothers, (being an unwed mother was a scandal in those days). She called her work "holy small deeds", pretty much what we would call *mitzvot* – a fundamental part of being Jewish.

For some, feminism and Judaism were conflicting ideas that couldn't live together.

For Bertha, feminism wasn't a threat to her Judaism. She worked hard to modernise the Jewish laws of marriage, divorce and inheritance. She knew that if more Jewish women learnt to speak in public, lead meetings and create organisations – in other words, become leaders – the Jewish nation would be strengthened – both the men and the women.

Bertha used not just deeds but a pen to try and change the world. She wrote bravely and boldly, but in those days, she couldn't always use her own name so for her translations of Bible into Yiddish, she used a pen name: Paul Berthold.

Perhaps her parents would have considered Paul the son they had hoped for? Or perhaps they would have seen Bertha as a person – whatever her gender – who had tried to make the world a better place, and had succeeded.

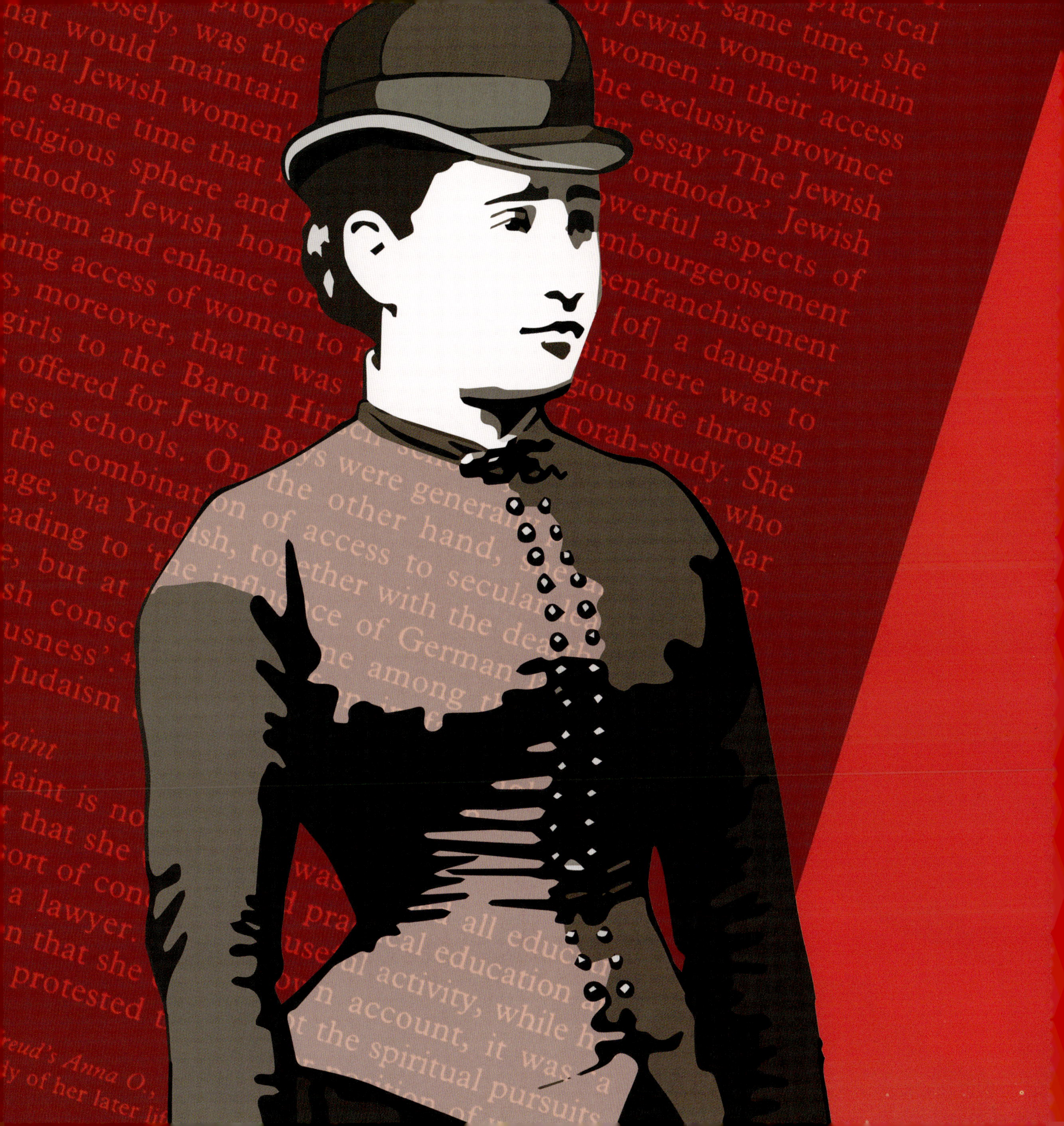

Helen

Helen Suzman
Human Rights Activist
South Africa
1917 - 2009

No blacks allowed. No coloureds* allowed. No Indians allowed. Whites only.

If you lived in South Africa between 1948 and 1994, this would not seem strange or unfair. For 50 years, apartheid – an Afrikaans word that means "separation" – had oppressed the people of colour in South Africa. Under apartheid, if you were not white, you were forced to live in separate areas from whites, use separate public facilities and get a different education. You were forced to carry a pass book to enter into "whites only" areas, and you had to obey curfew.

Although she was white (with all the privileges that came with it), this made Helen Suzman see red.

Like most Jewish South Africans, Helen's family had fled persecution from Russia. So they knew all about discrimination, but most were too afraid to speak up. Helen was not.

She became the only person in the (whites-only) South African Parliament to oppose apartheid. In fact, she was the only person in the opposition – her Progressive Party only managed to keep one seat in parliament from 1961 to 1974! Helen was quite literally, on her own. Her feeling of loneliness was worse, as she was an English-speaking Jewish woman in a parliament of mostly male Afrikaners, who spoke Afrikaans.

The famous Nelson Mandela wrote later: "It was an odd and wonderful sight to see this courageous woman peering into our cells and strolling around our (prison) courtyard. She was the first and only woman ever to grace our cells."

Although she was friendless, she refused to give in.

Although she had little support, Helen became one of the greatest human rights activists in South Africa.

For her courageous work, she was awarded honorary doctorates and awards, but perhaps Helen's greatest honour was being at Nelson Mandela's side in 1996 when he signed the new constitution, for a democratic and free South Africa.

Imagine having Nelson Mandela as your friend. Now that was a friend worth fighting for.

*Coloured - people of colour

"I stand for simple justice, equal opportunity and human rights ... well worth fighting for."

Helen Suzman

Edith

Edith Eger
Auschwitz survivor and Thriver of Life
Hungary, United States
1927 –

You always have a choice.

No matter your circumstances. No matter your loss. No matter your pain. You can choose calm and healing and joy. You can even dance.

This truth is what Edith Eger has lived, and a message that she has gifted the world.

Edith grew up in Hungary. She was a "normal" teenager, practicing to be a dancer, in love with her first boyfriend. She was even training to perform gymnastics at the upcoming Olympics. Then, in 1944, it all changed. The Nazis marched into Budapest, and she and her family were deported to Auschwitz. Surrounded by the awfulness of the camps, the evil SS officer Josef Mengele commanded Edith to dance for him. Dance? At a time and place like this? It seemed impossible.

But Edith closes her eyes. The familiar strains of music fill her ears. Her limbs feel heavy from terror, but *The Blue Danube* is a dance she can do in her sleep. She blocks the scary thoughts racing through her mind. The barrack's floor becomes the stage in the Budapest Opera House. Her drab prison garb transforms into a sparkly tutu. She imagines the flowers being thrown at her feet, the hushed audience. She dances and twirls, a high kick and then a pirouette.

She remembers her mother's advice – no-one can take from you what you've put in your mind.

It was these words that saved her life then, and would do so more times over.

"As a psychologist, mother, grandmother and great-grandmother, an observer of my own and others' behaviour and as an Auschwitz survivor, I am here to tell you that the worst prison is not the one the Nazis put me in. The worst prison is the one I built for myself."

- Excerpt from *The Choice*

And then she set about helping others with the "prisons" they had built for themselves. As a psychologist, she spent the next 40 years using her experience, as painful as it was, to heal herself and others.

We'll let her conclude:

"Though I could have remained a permanent victim – scarred by what was beyond my control– I made the choice to heal. Early on, I realised that true freedom can only be found by forgiving, letting go, and moving on. ... I have helped countless others lead full lives by moving beyond their problems – no matter how insurmountable they believed them to be. This is my life's mission and I will forever strive to help people make the choice to heal and thrive."

Anne

Not all stories have a happy ending. But, stories that people leave behind can be used to educate and inspire. Anne Frank's story is one of those.

Anne lived and went to school in Amsterdam. She had lots of friends, and spent her free time reading and playing table tennis. But when World War II broke out, life for Anne and her family became incredibly hard. The Nazis imposed strict rules on Jews, restricting the places they could visit, the shops they could use and even the schools they went to.

Scared for their lives, the Franks went into hiding, living for two years in a "Secret Annexe" behind a bookcase in the office building where Anne's father had worked. Heroic "helpers" brought the family food, clothing and other supplies while they were in hiding.

The family was joined by another – the Van Pels – and somehow they lived day after day in a cramped, three-storey space, having to be silent during the day when the workers were in the office, never going outdoors or meeting anyone else.

On her 13th birthday, Anne was given a diary that she named Kitty. Anne would write about everyday events in her diary; things that probably didn't seem that important at the time, but that have helped us form a picture of what life was like during this dark time in history.

She wrote about what she ate, the film stars that she admired, the books she read, and the arguments she would have with her mother. She also wrote about being in hiding, the fears and difficulties, and how she longed to go outside.

"Footsteps in the house, the private office, the kitchen, then ... on the staircase. All sounds of breathing stopped, eight hearts pounded ... Then we heard a can fall, and the footsteps receded. We were out of danger, so far!" – An extract from Anne's diary

Her last diary entry was August 1, 1940. It would be the end of Anne's life, but not the end of her story. Anne's diary was saved by one of the helpers, Miep. Since its publication, millions of copies have been sold around the world and it has been translated into more than 70 languages. It remains an important account of the treatment that Jewish people suffered at the hands of the Nazis – educating us all about the dangers of hatred, prejudice and discrimination.

Anne dreamed of wanting to become a famous writer, and indeed, she did.

She wrote:
"I want to be useful or bring enjoyment to all people, even those I've never met. I want to go on living even after my death! And that's why I'm so grateful to God for having given me this gift [of writing], which I can use to develop myself and to express all that's inside me!"

"In the long run, the sharpest weapon of all is a kind and gentle spirit."

Anne Frank

Bobbie

Bobbie Rosenfeld
super sportswoman and chocolate factory worker
Canada
1904 – 1969

Could anything be more fun than working in a chocolate factory?

Bobbie Rosenfeld could think of a few – hockey, basketball, softball, tennis and track.

During the workday, Canadian Olympic medallist Fanny "Bobbie" Rosenfeld was a stenographer in a Toronto chocolate factory, but in the evenings, she became "the world's best girl athlete."

On any given day she could be seen winning softball games before crowds of thousands, breaking national and international track records or leading an ice hockey or basketball team to a league championship.

Was there any sport Rosenfeld couldn't conquer? As one author remarked, "The most efficient way to summarise Bobbie Rosenfeld's career... is to say that she was not good at swimming."

Born in 1904 in what is now Ukraine, she gained the international spotlight with her achievements in track, bursting onto the scene at the 1923 Canadian National Exhibition. With a gold medal for the 400-metre relay, a silver for the 100-metre, and a fifth place in the 800-metre, Rosenfeld scored more points for her country than any other athlete at the Games, male or female.

An attack of severe arthritis forced her to retire permanently from athletics in 1933, so Bobbie then moved to coaching track and softball, and started writing about sports. Both as an athlete and then as a writer, Rosenfeld helped topple traditional barriers against women's participation in sports.

Amongst many honours, she was named Canada's Female Athlete of the First Half-Century (1900–1950), but perhaps her greatest achievements included her wisecracks and jokes, her bobbed haircut (hence her name) and her sportsmanship, er, sportswomanship.

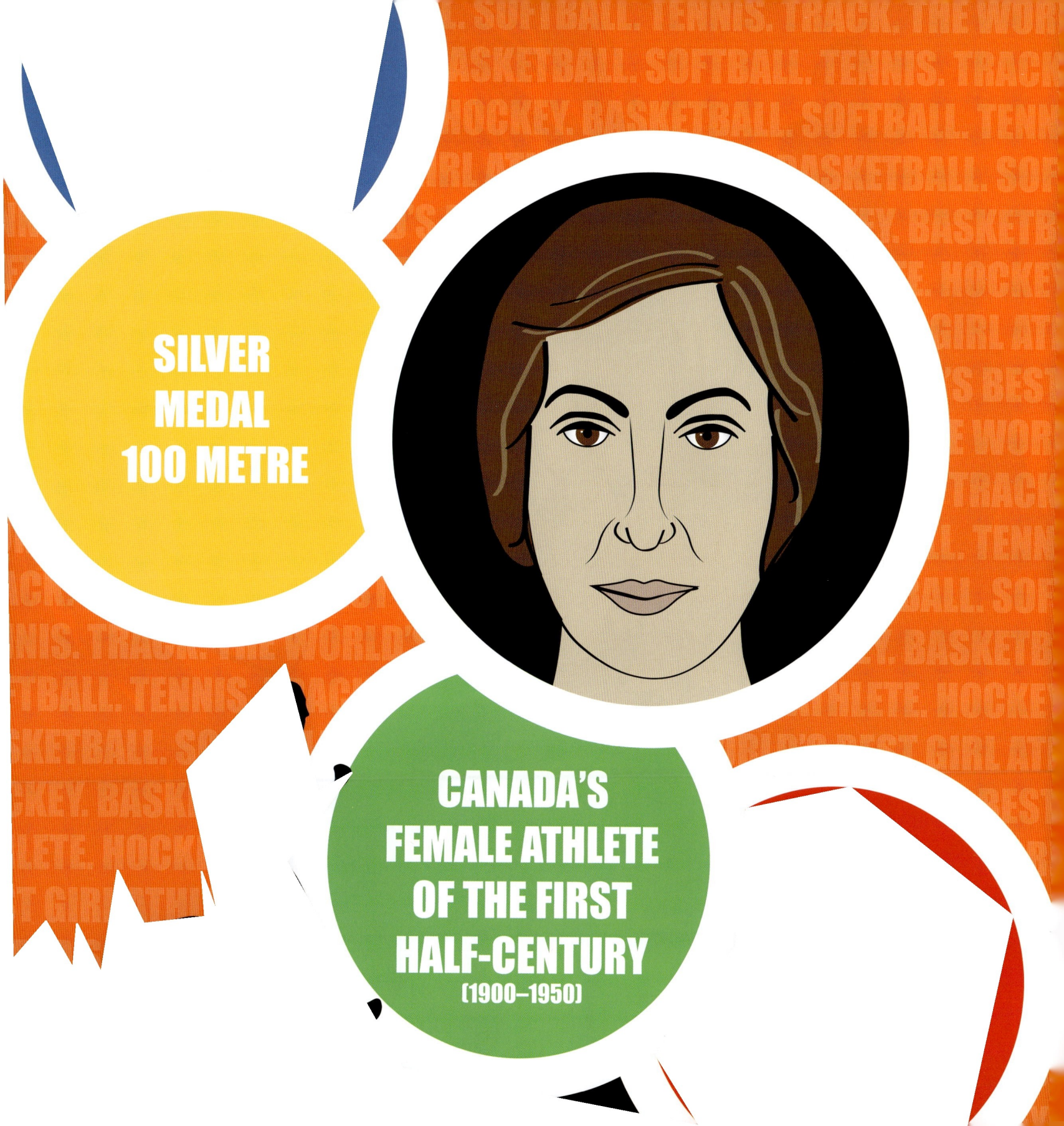

SILVER MEDAL 100 METRE

CANADA'S FEMALE ATHLETE OF THE FIRST HALF-CENTURY (1900–1950)

Donna

What's the comfiest, slouchiest, cosiest item in your wardrobe?

Most probably, whatever it is, it was inspired by Donna Karan's original collection – *The Essential's Line.*

Donna always said she would only design clothes that she could wear herself, and not just for fashion runway models. This made her the answer to most girls' and women's prayers!

Donna was born for this role, it seems. Her mother Helen ("Queenie") had been a model and worked in the showroom of famous fashion designer, Chester Weinberg, while her father had been a tailor and haberdasher (a person who sells men's clothing, or items to sew with).

At school, Donna was often to be found in the art department instead of in class ... but it was all to help her as she went on to Design School, an internship at Anne Klein's fashion house, and finally launching her own clothing company in 1985: Donna Karan New York.

Before Donna, there were strict rules about what you could wear and what you couldn't. The fashion world saw size four as the ideal size, but Donna wasn't interested in that. Her dream was "to design modern clothes for modern people." So she designed clothing for women who were beginning to go out to work in the male-dominated business world. She was so successful, she was nicknamed "The Queen of Seventh Avenue!"

Donna really did get "modern people", and that included the fact that good clothing was often more expensive than young women could afford. So in 1988, she extended her line by creating a less expensive clothing line for younger women, called – you guessed it – DKNY.

The lesson of this tale is that, if there is something you love and want, but it doesn't yet exist, make it happen! Donna has won many awards for her contribution to fashion, but in the end, matching what young women wanted and what she could give to the world was a perfect synchronicity. In fact, you could say that it was the perfect fit ...

Daughters of Zelophehad

It's awful to feel left out. But being excluded doesn't mean you have to stay that way, as the daughters of Zelophehad discover.

Five women sit on low stools inside a tent in the desert. It's thousands of years ago – years before the Suffragettes, aeons before the Women's Rights Movement. It's hot, it's dry… and they've been travelling with the rest of the Jewish people for 40 years. In the centre of the camp, land is being divided between the various tribes and clans within tribes – according to the law of the time, it is the men who will inherit the Land of Israel.

The five – Mahlah, Noah, Hoglah, Milcah, and Tirzah – look at one another. Their father, Zelophehad, one of the elders of the tribe of Menashe, has died, and left behind no sons. Only these daughters.

"Not good news for us, sisters. When a man dies, his property automatically goes to his sons. If there are no sons, the estate goes to brothers or parents. But not to us."

"And yet, we love the land of Israel! We want to be part of the destiny of its people! Is it fair, I ask you, that we are not to have a share? That our father's name and clan will disappear?"

"Let us go to Moses, and make our case."

"Do we dare?"

"Yes, for the love of the land."

These five go to the Tent of Meeting, and there, in front of all the elders, and the heads of tribes and clans, in front of Moses and Elazar the High Priest, they approach. Bravely, resolutely, they step forward to state their case: "Why should the name of our father disappear, just because he had no sons? Give us a portion along with our father's brothers."

Moses and the men are taken aback. They've never considered this before. But Moses realises that this is a big deal, and turns to God to find out the law.

"The plea of Zelophehad's daughters is correct!" announces God. "And more, here's an amendment to the law that takes the women into account and makes it official: If a man dies without leaving sons, you must transfer his property to his daughters."

It took pluck for the women to come forward, to stand up for what they believed to be true. And the story ends well for these five, as they did it for the right reasons and pure intentions. They loved their land, and they wanted to be a part of its legacy, and with a pure heart and cool head, they were.

Hedy

Hedy Lamarr
Hollywood Star and the Mother of WiFi
Austria, Germany, USA
1914 - 2000

Look at the cell phone in your hand. Your grandparents and parents will tell you that way back when, there was one (one!) phone in the house and it was attached to the wall with a wire or cord. And the receiver had to be attached to the base with another cord.

What if I told you that the reason you don't have to untangle those cords today is because of a movie star called Hedy Lamarr?

Hedy was born in Austria and moved to Germany where she became an actress, known as "the most beautiful woman in Europe". In the 1930s, she fled the country and her husband via London before arriving in America, where she became a Hollywood star.

At the same time though, Hedy was an inventor, always pottering with wires and bits of equipment. In fact, even on set she had an inventing table in her trailer in between takes!

But it was during World War II that Hedy felt she had to do more than act or just potter. So she teamed up with another unusual character – George Antheil, a music composer and inventor. Together they worked out how to "talk" to torpedoes so that they would hit their targets. The problem with torpedoes was that they had to be guided using radio waves, but these could be intercepted by the enemy. Hedy and George came up with the idea of "frequency hopping" – both transmitter and receiver would hop between frequencies, so that the torpedo could hit its target. They called it the "Secret Communications System" and offered it to the US Navy.

Unfortunately technology had to catch up to their invention, so the Navy never made use of it, but years later, it was key to the development of GPS (Global Positioning Systems), Bluetooth … and cell phones. So it is that Hedy Lamarr is known as "the mother of Wi-Fi".

"I can excuse everything but boredom. Boring people don't have to stay that way."

Hedy Lamarr

Belle

Belle Levy
Private Investigator
USA
1898 – 1978

In trouble? Need someone to track down a missing relative? Need something investigated – on the quiet? Then Belle Levy, P.I. (Private Investigator) and owner of Colonial Detective Service is your ma ... er woman.

Belle Levy, born in New York in 1898, certainly didn't start out as a private detective. She married at 17 and for a while designed children's clothes, until at 25 years old, she decided to do something almost no woman was doing at the time: she joined a detective agency. In this way, she became one of the first private investigators – male or female – to be licenced by the state of New York.

Belle clearly loved detecting – so much so that in 1927, she started her own agency – the Colonial Detective Service.

And she was good. No doubt about it. Her favourite method of investigating was to 'bump' into the person she was following as if by mistake, and then starting to talk to them. Sooner or later they'd tell her what she needed to know, and more.

Belle could get the goods alright. She cracked cases all across the US of A., and was so successful that she opened more offices in Manhattan and employed other women detectives across the country to help.

While she seems to have still been detecting, following leads and solving mysteries in 1958, what happened to her afterwards is just that – a mystery.

"My favourite cases? I like the ones with happy endings"

Sivan

Sivan Ya'ari
Environmental Innovator
Israel
1978 –

You're doing your homework, when you feel a little thirsty. So you go to the kitchen and switch on the tap, and clear, cold water gushes into your glass. You toss it back without a thought.

You are still doing your homework (bear with us here) and as night falls, you cannot see the page you're reading. Without thinking, you reach up and flick the switch. Light floods your room.

But what if you had no access to light or water? What if you had to take a bucket and walk a mile down to a muddy, crocodile-infested river to get water? What if you only had a candle, its flickering flame too small for you to read by?

This is what 20-year-old Sivan saw when she went on holiday to Africa: "I saw people and children looking for water, physically digging for it with their hands, because the water is underground, and in order to get to the water they have to pump it out. But in order to pump it out, they need electricity."

There are more than 600 million people in Africa who have no electricity, which means that many have no water either. Sivan decided to do something about it. She began with one village in Tanzania: she brought solar panels from Israel and put them up on the roof of a clinic. With the electricity, medicines could be stored in a refrigerator, and nurses and doctors could care for patients at night – not by the light of a candle but by the light of technology. Most importantly, clean water could be pumped from under the ground.

In 2010, Sivan took the idea further, creating a company called Innovation: Africa – which has a simple goal: to bring the wonders of Israeli technology to Africa, one village at a time.

Here's how you do this: First, drill deep down into the earth until you find water. Then, put a solar panel on a roof or somewhere nice and sunny and attach it to a solar collector and a pump. The energy from the sun powers the pump, which draws water up into a large tank. Now lay down pipes and connect them to taps or faucets at different places in the village. Finally, watch as you turn on the tap – and water spurts out to the sound of the children singing: "Welcome, Israel! Welcome, Israel!"

In this way, not only do all have clean water to drink, but students can study, farmers can farm, nurses can nurse, and everyone can live healthier, better lives.

Slowly but surely, one village at a time, Sivan has reached one million people in 10 African countries.

So you see, you don't need a complicated plan to change the world.

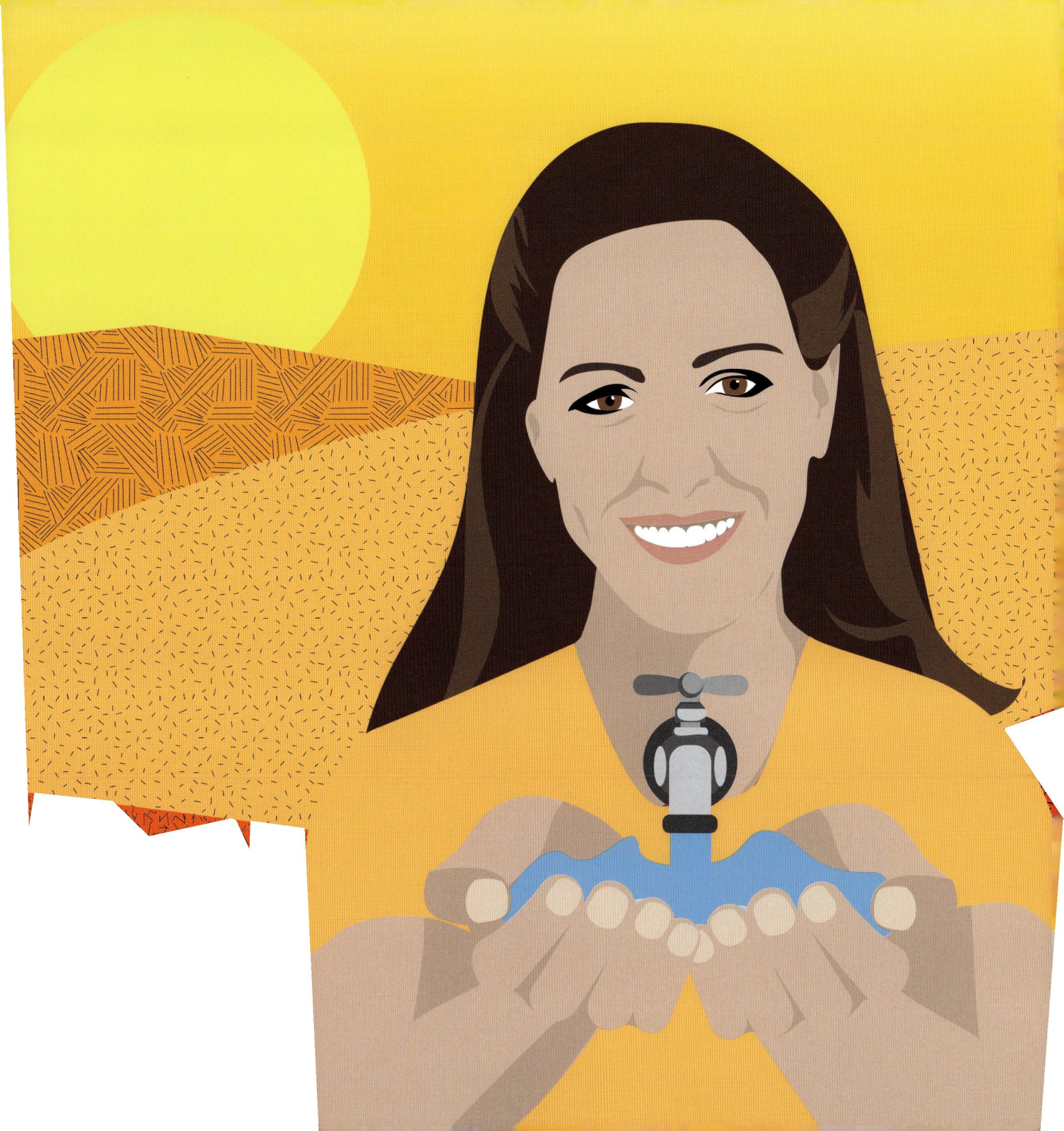

"We are committed to bring water where there is drought, to bring light where there is darkness, to bring hope and dignity where there is despair."

Sivan Ya'ari

Hannah

Be brave. Act, even if you feel scared.

The story of Hannah Senesh is the story of a girl who was courageous in the scariest of circumstances.

Hannah grew up in Budapest in a family that wasn't very interested in being Jewish. But, when fellow students bullied her because she was a Jew, instead of feeling fear, (although I am sure she did) she thought to herself, "Okay, I want to find out what this Jewish thing is all about."

So she learnt about Zionism – the Jewish dream to return to its homeland from which it had been exiled 2000 years before. It made such an impression of her, that she made *Aliyah** in 1939.

Meanwhile, the war was raging in Europe. Wherever the Nazis conquered, they sent the Jews to concentration camps and to death. Jews all around the world felt fear, but Hannah thought, "How can I help?"

So she volunteered to take part in a top-secret mission: to parachute behind enemy lines and help the Jews trapped there. To do this, she had to learn how to parachute and how to use a transmitter radio, which would send coded messages back to the British.

Imagine Hannah standing at the exit doorway of that plane, about to jump. Heart thumping in her chest, her mouth dry,

land miles and miles below her and enemies in wait ... She must have been so scared, but still she took the leap.

She was captured almost at once, and because she had a transmitter radio, the Hungarian police tortured her cruelly for months to get the codes from her. But she refused to give them up. Instead, she dished up defiance. Five months later, a trial was held, where Hannah promised the judges that they would soon be judged themselves. The head officer was furious at this impudence, and on the morning of November 7, 1944, cruelly gave her a choice: beg for a pardon or face death by firing squad.

Hannah must have been terrified, but did not back down from what she knew as truth. Hannah chose death, refusing a blindfold and facing her murderers across the snow. She was 23 years old.

Hannah is one of modern Israel's greatest heroes, and will be remembered forever. Not because she wasn't scared in the worst of situations, but because she was scared and took action anyway.

The words of one of her famous poems captures it:
The voice called, and I went.
I went, because the voice called.

*to make Aliyah is to go to live in Israel

Sheyna

Sheyna Gifford
Astronaut and cool scientist
USA
1979-

Do you dream of going to space?

Sheyna Gifford does. Sheyna is a physician, a neuroscientist, and a writer, but her favourite thing to do is to pretend she's on Mars. Which is not as easy as it sounds. She is a *simulated astronaut* – someone who practices living and working in space, so that when we finally go there, we know what to expect. We need to know how to live where there is no air, water or food, and what to do if things go wrong.

Sheyna and five others were selected from hundreds of candidates for the mission, known as HI-SEAS (which stands for Hawai'i Space Exploration Analog and Simulation) and squeezed into a dome on a barren lava field on the slopes of a volcano in Hawaii. Sheyna worked as the team's doctor and also its journalist, blogging of their adventures "all the way" from Mars.

In an area the size of a small two-bedroom home, the team lived, worked, slept and ate for 366 days in a row. In order to make it as real as possible, they couldn't speak to anyone outside the dome in real time, they had no access to fresh food aside from what they could grow, and they never went more than two kilometres (a mile) away from the dome – and only in a spacesuit. No fresh air for a year, think of that!

It turns out that what astronauts today need to know is more than science and maths. They need to know how to cook, clean, repair stuff and, above all, how to get on with others in a small confined space. As Sheyna puts it, their mission was: "Go to Mars, grow food, do science, don't kill each other."

It's not just science, she says. It's how to live.

What Sheyna learnt was that living is living, no matter where you are, and personal values will apply as much as ever.

"Being a Jew is a community activity, a group effort. Any individual work you do, such as being a thoughtful, contemplative and helpful person, you do in the context of the whole world".

I always wanted to be an astronaut, because being an astronaut is being a hero, a leader, having the ability to spread the word about how cool science is.

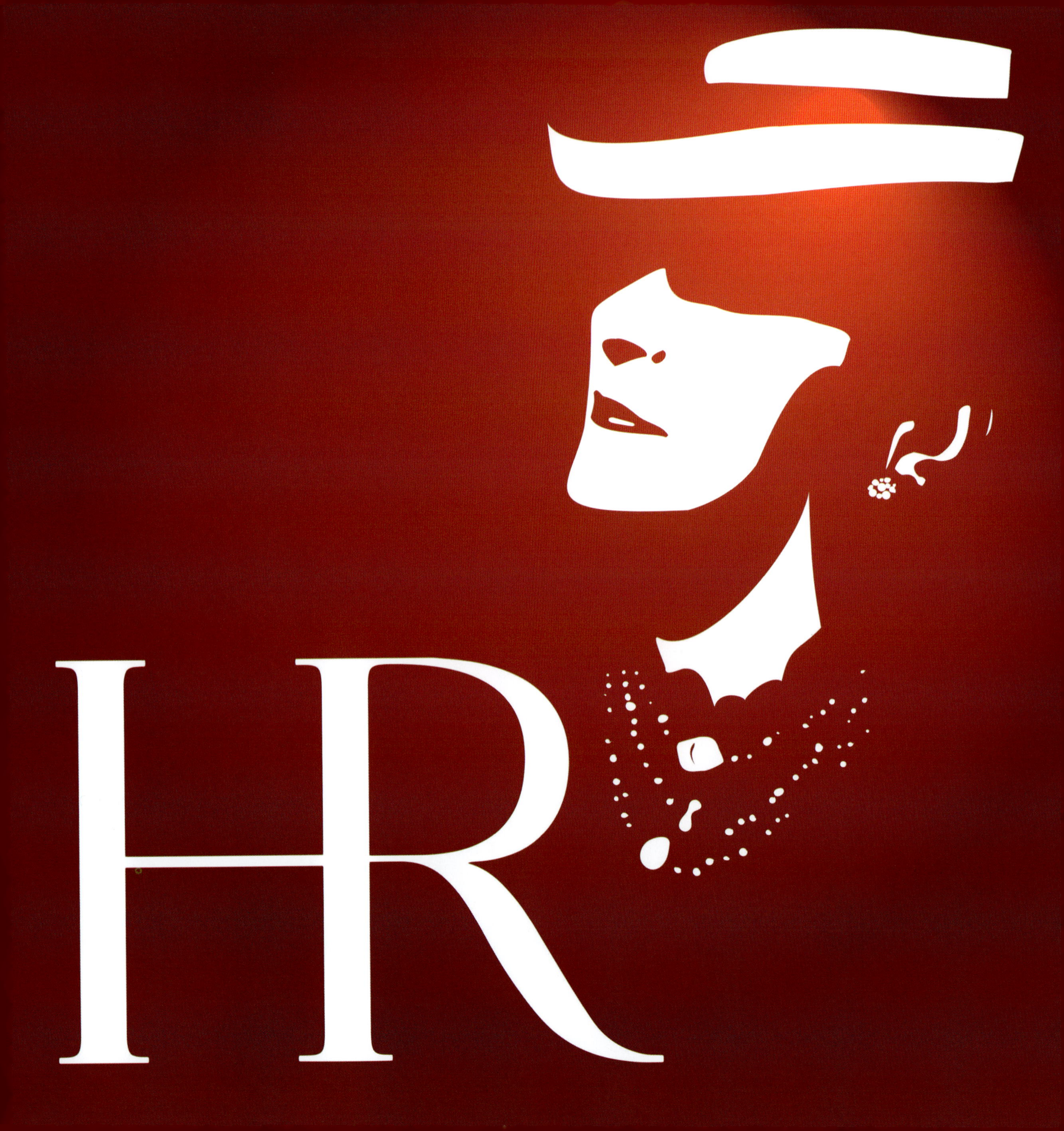
HR

Helena

Beauty is for everyone.

Short and "built like an icebox," Helena Rubinstein was not who you'd choose to advertise beauty. But in fact, that made her the perfect proof: If she could change herself by sheer effort into prettiness personified, so could her clients. In clothes by the finest Paris couturiers and the sparkliest of jewels, her face made up to perfection and dark hair wrapped tightly around her head, she proved that it wasn't what you were born with that counted, but what you did with it.

Unlike her arch-rival, Elizabeth Arden, Helena believed that looking pretty was not a luxury. Anyone could do it. There were no ugly women, Rubinstein said, "only lazy ones."

Helena, born in Poland, was helping her father at business meetings by the age of 15. When he insisted she marry a man twice her age, she refused and jumped on a boat to Australia with no money and little English. She did have a few jars of the cream that her beautiful mother used in her luggage though…

When Australian ladies saw her pink and white complexion next to theirs, she began to sell the jars to them. When she ran out, she began to create her own. One of the most important ingredients in her new cream was lanolin, which come from sheep; luckily, in Australia, there are plenty of sheep. It smelt a bit though, so Helena did experiments in her kitchen using lavender and pine bark to disguise the smell. To sound fancy, she called it a false French name and *voila*!

But Helena didn't need a fake name. It wasn't long before she opened her own cosmetics company called simply: Helena Rubinstein, Beauty Salon. After eight successful years, she returned to Europe and opened salons in Paris and London. She invented new creams and studied further, always learning and pushing herself further.

In 1915, Helena and her then-husband arrived in New York. Here, women were taking charge of their lives and throwing aside their corsets. Helena urged them to take charge of their appearance as well.

A clever businesswoman, Helena showed that beauty could also make you financially independent – even rich. She sold her business to Lehman Brothers, the famous banking house, but when she saw they weren't running it well, during the stock market crash of 1929, she bought it back at a fraction of the price. In 1941, when she wanted to rent an apartment on Park Avenue, the landlord refused because he didn't want a Jewish tenant. So she bought the whole block.

Helena lived large. She commissioned art by Salvador Dali and rugs by Joan Miro. She wore the best in clothing and jewellery, established scholarships and foundations and even married a prince. But "Madame", as she was called, always took a packed lunch to work and worked even when she was ill. As she said, "Hard work keeps the wrinkles out of the mind and spirit."

Gertrude

Gertrude Elion
Nobel Prize-winner and pickle-scientist
USA
1918 - 1999

Dill or Garlic. Sweet or sour. Pickle flavours are hardly "save the world stuff". But the time Gertrude Elion spent in food laboratories testing pickles and mayonnaise was just the learning time she needed. She went on to become one of the most important biochemists in the world, and her work truly saved countless lives. You see, saving the world has to start somewhere.

Gertrude Belle Elion had a good life, growing up in a lovely big apartment in Manhattan. But, in 1929, the stock market crashed. Like many others, Gertrude's family lost most of their money, and life for the Elions crashed too.

When Gertrude's beloved grandfather died of cancer, it planted a seed in her that became her dream – to become a chemist and work towards finding a cure for the disease.

But, there was no money for luxuries or new clothes or fancy food, or things like higher education. Gertrude worked hard and, with her good grades, got into Hunter's College, which was free. After graduating from college, the next hurdle was graduate school – something her family simply could not afford. This time, good grades weren't going to help.

Work prospects were bleak. Employment was scarce for everyone during the Great Depression, and anyway, many couldn't accept the idea that a woman could be a good chemist.

Then World War II broke out, and suddenly everything changed. With men joining the fighting forces *en masse,* many more jobs became available to women. Suddenly, Gertrude could get a job with food manufacturer Quaker Maid, and, yes, started off testing the acidity of pickles and quality control of mayonnaise.

From there, she went on to become a highly respected biochemist and pharmacologist at medical research laboratories, until her death at the age of 81. Along the way, she received three honorary doctorate degrees and won the Nobel Prize in Medicine in 1988 for her research and creation of many critically important drugs to treat leukaemia, malaria, and a drug that makes transplant surgery possible till today.

People ask me often: (was) the Nobel Prize the thing you were aiming for all your life? And I say that would be crazy. Nobody would aim for a Nobel Prize because, if you didn't get it, your whole life would be wasted. What we were aiming at was getting people well, and the satisfaction of that is much greater than any prize you can get.

"Don't be afraid of hard work. Nothing worthwhile comes easily. Don't let others discourage you or tell you that you can't do it. In my day, I was told women didn't go into chemistry. I saw no reason why we couldn't."

Gertrude Elion

Gracia

Whatever superpower you have, use it for good.

For the 16th-century Jewish businesswoman, Dona Gracia Nasi, hers was, hers was wealth and power. Because of who she was, she rubbed shoulders with kings and queens, took on the Pope, and saved countless Jews from persecution across Europe.

These were dark days for the Jewish people. Wherever the Spanish Empire reached, the Inquisition* followed. Jews were forced to convert to Christianity or leave the country. Some Jews did convert, but others continued to practice Judaism in secret. This was very dangerous – if these "*conversos*" or crypto-Jews were caught, they were tortured and killed. As a *converso*, "Beatrice Mendez", Gracia was a Jew in secret.

When her father and husband died, she also became the head of a tremendously wealthy spice business – the most powerful in Europe. But having money didn't stop the Inquisition from chasing her. She had to flee Portugal, and eventually she had to leave Christian lands completely, ending her days in Muslim Constantinople.

Fleeing your home is a scary thing, and because she knew exactly what it felt like, Gracia used her money to secure safe passage for fleeing *conversos*, and supported them as they started new lives. She used her power to speak up against the powerful Pope Paul IV when he arrested Jewish merchants and confiscated their wealth. She even bought the town of Tiberias on the shore of the Sea of Galilee from the Turks, wanting to create a refuge for *conversos*.

Over her lifetime, Gracia gained other names, not just her Christian one – like "our angel" and "the heart of the people". But the Jews she saved and their descendants call her "Doña" or "La Senora" – The Lady.

Across the ages, Dona Gracia showed us the real power of money and influence – to save and change lives.

*Inquisition: People and institutions within the Catholic Church whose aim was to combat what they saw was heresy – beliefs that went against their own.

Emma

Open arms mean an open heart. The kind of welcome you receive when visiting new friends or a new city or even a new country can make a big difference.

Even though Emma came from a wealthy family, her parents were Jewish immigrants who were forced to flee their Russian home. She knew what it meant to leave a place where you were hated, and to come to a place that promised you freedom.

She was openly proud of being Jewish, and she was deeply troubled by the dangers faced by her fellow Russian Jews. She also spoke up against the anti-Semitism and terrible conditions that many Russian refugees lived in when they finally got to America. She felt that Jews needed to help all those suffering and in need, saying: "Until we are all free, we are none of us free."

In 1883, France shipped over an enormous statue called "Liberty Enlightening the World" to New York as a gift. But it didn't come with a pedestal, so the Americans had to make one themselves. To help raise funds for this, famous authors and artists were asked to donate some form of art to be auctioned off. Emma was a well-known poet by this time, and was asked to write a sonnet. She didn't really want to write a "poem for order" (artists often don't like that!), but she did it to help a friend.

And because she had something important to say.

The Statue of Liberty is huge. It stands out and dominates the skyline of New York. It is dramatic and even intimidating. But the poem on the bronze tablet at the entrance was Emma's word-version of open arms – a warm welcome to everyone and anyone coming to America.

Her words changed the way people saw a statue, and made it a symbol of hope, freedom, justice, and the power that each person holds.

The New Colossus

Not like the brazen giant of Greek fame,

With conquering limbs astride from land to land;

Here at our sea-washed, sunset gates shall stand

A mighty woman with a torch, whose flame

Is the imprisoned lightning, and her name

Mother of Exiles. From her beacon-hand

Glows world-wide welcome; her mild eyes command

The air-bridged harbour that twin cities frame.

"Keep, ancient lands, your storied pomp!" cries she

With silent lips. "Give me your tired, your poor,

Your huddled masses yearning to breathe free,

The wretched refuse of your teeming shore.

Send these, the homeless, tempest-tost to me,

I lift my lamp beside the golden door!"

Emma Lazarus, written in 1883

Sarah

Sarah Schenirer
Girls' School pioneer
Poland
1883 – 1935

There are days when we don't want to go to school. "Whyyyy," we whine, "do we need to go to school?"

What if we couldn't, though? What if girls couldn't go to school? Not so long ago this was the case. In the early 20th century, there were no schools where girls could learn about being Jewish or even some Torah. Until one young woman changed history for us.

You must remember that this went against hundreds of years of tradition, where girls learnt from their mothers; often they didn't know how to read or write, or if they did, it was in Yiddish, not Hebrew. But Sarah was not afraid (or maybe a bit).

Sarah went to elementary school – and was teased by her friends for wanting to study more. Her father rolled his eyes, but allowed her to study with him. She became a seamstress, but at night, she would delve into Jewish studies, Polish and German literature, history and education – anything really, by the light of a candle.

She was bothered that the young Jewish women she saw around her were not interested in their own heritage, they didn't know much about it. Having gone to state schools, they knew more about Polish and "secular" subjects than their own, and they were turning away from their tradition.

So one day in 1917, in a small room in Krakow, Sarah gathered seven young girls around her and began to teach. She taught Hebrew and Torah, and her pupils loved it so much that what began as a small school became a movement.

Sarah called it Bais Yaacov (based on a verse in Exodus, where Moses tells "the House of Jacob" to draw near to hear the Ten Commandments) and within five years it had grown to seven schools with over a thousand students. By 1933, there were 265 schools in Poland alone – for some 38 000 students!

Sarah didn't just open a school. She opened minds.

Rosanna

Rosanna Dyer Osterman
Inventor biscuit-baker and philanthropist
United States
1809 – 1866

Did I ever tell you about Rosanna Osterman? No? Come, sit at the fire with me, under the Texan stars and I'll tell you. Here, try one of these biscuits, they're her recipe! A bit dry, you say? Yes, well, that's the point, isn't it? You see, Rosanna invented these biscuits that would never spoil, so that people on the frontier could explore and travel without running out of food. And that was just one thing Rosanna did.

Rosanna first arrived in Galveston, Texas, in 1838 with her husband, and together they set up a general store. They were wealthy, sure – in fact they built the first two-storey residence in the town.

But there's more, I tell you. Rosanna wasn't just a rich businesswoman.

She was shocked when she learnt that there was nowhere to bury Mr Abrahams who had died of yellow fever, so she brought a Rabbi out to consecrate a Jewish cemetery – in the middle of what was nowhere at the time.

She was someone who cared for the sick and dying. Why, during the terrible yellow fever epidemic of '53, she built a temporary hospital on her own land, and brought the sick there to recover.

She did the same thing in the Civil War and looked after soldiers on both sides of the fight. She tore up her sheets for bandages and her plush carpets became slippers!

Her death was as dramatic as her life; she died in a steamboat explosion on the Mississippi River ...

As exciting as her life sounds, you can tell what was important to her, can't you? People.

She helped people, nursed them, created communities, founded synagogues. She saw her life – and her wealth – as just there to help make the world a better place.

Why, after she died, all her money – she had left $200 000, which was a humungous sum in those days – went to so many charities all over the US that they said of her: "The history of Rosanna Osterman is more eloquently written in the untold charities that have been dispensed by her liberal hands than any eulogy man can bestow."

What's in the biscuits? I thought you'd never ask. There's dried, powdered buffalo meat, beans, and cornmeal. Yum!

Asenat

Asenat Barzani
First Female spiritual leader and Iraqi poet
Southern Kurdistan, Iraq
1590 – c. 1670

Ew kata bash*! Salaam alaikum. Let me introduce myself.

I am the Torah teacher from Amedi you have heard so much about. I am blessed to be the leader of the Yeshiva and an instructor to so many students. Can you picture me? Long flowing robes and head scarf, pretty face, beautiful hair, nose ring and delicate fingers ...

Were you expecting me to say – manly features and a long beard?

Well, my father looked like that when he ran the Yeshiva. But I was very lucky that my father educated me as he would a son, even though that was certainly not done for other girls. So even when I married, even in a traditional Kurd marriage, it was accepted that I continue my studies and my holy work.

From the start, my Rabbi husband was involved in his studies and did not have time to teach the students, so I would teach them instead, like a helpmate. Lucky I did, because when my husband died, I took over the yeshiva myself, teaching those who had come for rabbinic training.

I am what they call a *Tanna'it* – the female version of a *Tannai* – the word for a Talmudic scholar par excellence. I may not have been a Rabbi formally, but I certainly fulfilled all the requirements and was looked up to by everyone in the community of Mosul, becoming its spiritual leader.

There are many stories about the miracles that surrounded me.

In one, I persuaded the whole community of the shul of Amedi to join me outdoors to celebrate Rosh Chodesh – the New Moon – when someone set the shul on fire. Although no-one was inside, thank God, there were holy books and the Torah that were being burnt. Panic and despair filled the air. I had to do something! I whispered a secret name of God – and lo and behold, a flock of angels descended on the shul and put out the fire. In thanks, the shul was renamed after me and still stands in the town of Amedi to this day.

Some say I was the first female rabbinical leader ever, and that may be true, but, dear reader, I know for sure that I will not be the last.

*Greetings in Kurdish

Ester

There is a Jewish concept that "Bishvili nivrahhaolam – for me, the world was created."

Everything in your life – where you live, who your family is, and even what you look like – all of this is set up just so you can realise your dreams, learn and grow from your mistakes, and become the best person you can be. But that also means that you have a responsibility to use all the good stuff you have, or the stuff you don't have, to make your mark on the world.

Once upon a time, in a city called Shushan, there was a girl called Ester, who was chosen by Achashverosh, the Persian King, to be his queen. Now you would think that being queen is the best thing ever – beautiful clothes, servants all around, a magnificent palace. But Queen Ester had a secret – she was Jewish. And King Achashverosh had an advisor who he trusted most, the evil Haman, who hated Jews. That made being Queen a dangerous place to be.

One day, Ester's uncle Mordechai refused to bow down to the advisor Haman. Haman was incensed, and in revenge, hatched a hateful plan to kill all the Jews of the Shushan. The Jews were terrified and did not know where to turn. And here was Ester, the Jewish Queen, in the palace of the King - in the perfect place with the perfect title to rescue her people!

But Ester was scared. It was against the law of the land to approach the King without being summoned – even if you were the Queen. She was full of fear, but Ester knew she had to step up. Perhaps it was for this reason alone that God made her Queen of Persia in the first place? She asked all the Jews of Shushan to fast and pray with her. Summoning all her courage, she invited the King and Haman to a banquet, and in the middle of the sumptuous meal, revealed Haman's evil plot to kill her and her people. Achashverosh was furious, and immediately set to punish Haman and overthrow the dastardly plot. The Jews were saved! Ester had done it!

Since then, the story of Ester – Megillat Ester – is read on Purim, a festival where Jews all around the world celebrate the miraculous escape from Haman's evil decree with dressing up, feasting and sharing food gifts with friends.

Ester is undoubtedly the heroine of this miraculous story. But did knowing that all the Jews of Shushan were behind her give her strength? Had God been her help? Had all the details of her life worked together to set the stage so that she could fulfil her destiny to become the famous Queen Ester of the Purim story?

It was Ester who insisted that her story be written for Jews through the ages. Perhaps she knew that the questions are as relevant now as they were those thousands of years ago? Either way, she is the inspiration that reminds us to become the heroines of our own stories.

Ester is the inspiration that reminds us to become the heroines of our own stories.

Sarah

Scene I: Sarah Bernhardt's dressing room.

SARAH enters, *leaning on a cane, stage left and sits down at a mirror.*

SARAH:

Imagine a world without television or Facebook. A world where there is only the stage. The whole world's a stage, as Shakespeare said. Yes, I played many roles, including his.

"The divine Sarah" they called me.

She rises and limps to the front of the stage.

SARAH:

I was born illegitimate, Henriette Rosine Bernard, but changed my name to the biblical Sarah. I rubbed my Jewishness in the faces of the anti-Semites who loved and hated me. They accused me of sounding "like a Jew"! But, I told them, "I am a daughter of the great Jewish race, and my somewhat uncultivated language is the outcome of our enforced wanderings". So I transformed myself from a wandering Jew – such a dreadful cliché! – into an international star who travelled the world – and enchanted it.

I pushed my power and independence; I didn't care what people thought. When they said I had a big nose, I made sure my portraits were in profile. When they said my hair was frizzy, I refused to straighten it. They all said I was too thin. So I wore tight dresses.

SARAH climbs onto the box, her head raised theatrically and her arm outstretched.

I made my first appearance at the French National Theatre in 1862. I've played all the great parts there are – from tragic heroines to queens, even men: Shakespeare's Hamlet was one of my finest performances if I say so myself. When I was 45, I played a 19-year-old girl.

Oh, they loved me. Not for my beauty, but for my stage presence. It was my expressive voice and my emotional acting that did it. I knew precisely how to place myself on a stage to create the perfect picture – you could say I was the forerunner of Instagram.

MARK TWAIN enters stage right; moves to side, turns to SARAH and declaims:

There are five types of actresses: bad actresses, fair actresses, good actresses, great actresses – and then there is Sarah Bernhardt.

Exit stage left.

SARAH smiles – clearly aware of her audience:

I had kings sending me jewels, gentlemen fighting over me with swords. Priests thought I was evil, but my fans adored me. I wrote poetry and books, and ran theatre companies.

I had to have my leg amputated in 1905, you know, but that didn't stop me. I couldn't move around the stage so well, but my "golden voice" captivated people all over the world.

Lights dim.

When I take my final bow, all they'll put on my tombstone is my name: Sarah Bernhardt. There is no need for anything more. After all, who doesn't love a drama queen?

The crowd in front roars, leaps to its feet shouting, throwing roses at her feet:
SARAH, SARAH!

SARAH exits, stage left.

"My life has been a struggle - a struggle to have my own way where I felt I was in the right."

Sarah Bernhardt

Ruth

"Fight for the things that you care about. But do it in a way that leads others to join you."

Disagreeing is sometimes hard to do. Maybe some won't like you if you don't agree with their ideas. Others will think you are crabby for not towing the line. You may even be persecuted or put into jail for not agreeing with others. But Ruth Bader Ginsburg proves that, "You can disagree without being disagreeable."

When Ruth was growing up, she noticed the world had rules like: "No Jews or dogs allowed!" Parks that were for whites only. No Mexicans. No coloureds. Men only. At the time, girls were expected to find husbands and have babies, nothing else. But Ruth did not agree. It was acceptable for girls to become teachers or nurses, but certainly not to study law. Ruth did not agree. More than anything she wanted to do something that could fight prejudice and injustice, make the world a fairer place.

In a Law class of nine women and five hundred men, Ruth studied as hard as she could, but on graduating, no-one would hire her. Why not? She was a girl, a Jew and a mother. In this world of rules, that made her unsuitable in every way. But that did not stop her.

Ruth was eventually hired by a judge who gave her a chance, and she went on to fight for equal opportunities for women in the Supreme Court. She argued that in the same way women were being unfairly excluded from the workplace, men were being excluded from home and family life. In their house, her husband Martin cooked the meals while she went to work. People thought that was strange, but she disagreed. She did not win every case, but slowly and surely, things began to change.

Ruth became an outstanding lawyer, and in 1993, she was sworn in as the first Jewish woman Justice in the highest court of the land – the Supreme Court. To inspire herself, she had an important Jewish teaching hanging in her court chambers: *"Tzedek, tzedek tirdof* – Justice, justice you shall pursue" (Devarim/Deuteronomy 16:20).

Ruth was famous for her collection of jabots, a special collar worn over her robe. "The standard robe is made for a man because it has a place for the shirt to show, and the tie". Ruth wanted something more feminine for her robe.

She was also famous for changing her jabot according to her opinion. When she wanted to express approval, she wore her yellow jabot or her favourite beaded one from Cape Town. To express disapproval, her jabot was armour-like – perfect for dissent.

"My mother told me to be a lady. And for her, that meant be your own person, be independent."

Ruth Bader Ginsburg

Gisèle

Today we have selfies. We stretch our arms out as far as they can go, and we put on a smile for the camera embedded in our mobile phones.

Gisèle also took selfies – called self-portraits – along with portraits of many other people throughout her life. But, for her, it was more than a photo. With a picture, she tried to capture the whole person, the essence of the thinking and feeling human being in front of her. And that made her photos as alive as the subjects themselves.

Like your mobile never leaves your side, Gisèle's camera never left hers.

So her life journey was captured too. She began to take pictures of what was going on in Germany during the rise of Nazism, and eventually fled over the border to France with just that camera and some photographic negatives hidden strapped to her body.

She continued studying at the Sorbonne, but, as the Nazis marched into Paris, she again had to run, living underground for two years in the south of France. She managed to escape to Argentina, next moving to Mexico.

Her camera didn't just shoot the world events around her, but the truth. Sometimes truth is hard to see, and that upset a good number of people.

The photos she took of Evita Peron in Argentina upset so many people that she had to escape that country too, with the negatives hidden on her body again! She eventually returned to France and lived there for the rest of her life, photographing people and writing books about photography.

Gisèle is considered to be one of the greatest photographers ever. She was the first woman to receive France's most prestigious award in photography, the Grand Prix National des Photography – in 1980.

Taking photos of events and people was how she made her living, but using her lens to hone in on the core of events and people was her superpower.

If Gisèle took your portrait, what would she discover about you?

"When you do not like human beings, you cannot make good portraits."

Gisèle Freund

Emmy

1900:

It's no fun being the only girl in class who loves maths. To me, numbers, equations and theorems are simply beautiful. I do so want to be a mathematician like my father!

1901

They finally allowed me into the University of Erlangen to study mathematics. But not for credit, because the university doesn't allow women in. I won't give up until I get that degree.

1907:

Not only did I get my degree, but I now have a PhD – I am (wait for it…) a doctor of maths!

1908:

I have begun teaching, but still, I am not paid or have an official title. It seems the (male) lecturers said: "What will our soldiers think when they return to the university and find that they are required to learn at the feet of a woman?"

1910:

I have begun to play with the concept of "abstract algebra" – instead of real numbers, I look at the structures and concepts behind them. This is a new idea that I am helping to shape.

1915:

Despite being a woman, my (unofficial) colleagues, Felix Klein, and David Hilbert, have given me an incredible opportunity: to look at Einstein's brilliant new General Theory of Relativity and connect it to algebra.

1918:

I've seen the universe through the eyes of pure numbers – and it is beautiful. I've discovered that there are links between time and energy, between mathematics and physics – how the world works. Not bad for a female.

1933:

All this time I have continued to teach and even got paid eventually, although still without being called professor, because I'm a woman and a Jewish one at that. Now the Nazis have risen to power and they've fired me. I leave for the free world tonight.

Emmy fled the Nazis to the US where she continued to teach her favourite subject.

Her work on Einstein's theory is known today as Noether's Theorem*, changing the way scientists looked at the world. And it is even more wondrous than we imagined.

*Theorem – a statement that is proven to be true by other accepted truths or previously established statements.

"In the judgment of the most competent living mathematicians, Fraulein Noether was the most significant creative mathematical genius thus far..."

Albert Einstein, 1935

Glückel

My dear children, I write you this in case today or tomorrow your children or grandchildren do not know about their family. I have put it down briefly so that you may know from what kind of people you are descended.

Today we have bloggers. In the 18th century, memoirs were all the rage. A memoir, like it sounds, is a book filled with memories of one's life. Most European Jewish women in the 1700s would have little to say in their diaries (if they could write at all, that is), but Glückel was different. She was a businesswoman, married twice and had 12 children!

Glückel started writing her memoirs in Yiddish when she was 46, after her husband died, to share the story of the family with her children. She begins by describing her spiritual world, giving her children "*mussar*" – the ethics and morals of a religious Jew.

She then looks back at her childhood and "teenage" years, showing us how it came to be that she could write: her father made sure that both his daughters and sons were educated. Then:

My father had me betrothed when I was a girl of barely twelve, and less than two years later I married ... There I was, a carefree child whisked in the flush of youth from my parents, friends, and everyone I knew, from a city like Hamburg into a back-country town [Hameln] where only two Jews lived.

A year later, the couple moved to Hamburg, where her husband worked buying and selling gold. By 15 years old, Glückel was pregnant – at the same time as her mother and both gave birth within a week of one another ... something Glückel seems to have gotten a kick out of. While she went on to give birth to 14 children (two of whom died), she also got involved in trade and was so good at it, that she was a full partner in the family business. She remarks that when it came to business decisions, "my husband did nothing without my knowledge".

After her husband died, Glückel further sharpened her skills and traded in gems and finance, and travelled Europe as a businesswoman. She even opened a sock factory! In her writings, she takes pride in marrying off all her children – an important element of Jewish life in those times.

She married a second time, a banker, but it turned out he wasn't so good at holding onto money and Glückel ended her days penniless, living with one of her daughters.

Her writing is not only about her own life, however. Glückel wrote about things that happened in her community, or town, or in the village or city that she happened to be doing business in. She remarked on anything that she felt had a lesson for her children, or that interested her, from the wars between Germany and France, to the arguments in the shul of Meltz.

We are given a peep into a whole society – real life – in the 1700s, thanks to Glückel opening the window for us.

Pramila

Esther Victoria Abraham (Pramila)
Bollywood Star
Mumbai India
1916 – 2006

A Jewish Bollywood star – seriously? Esther Victoria Abraham – known by her stage name Pramila – was a fearless stunt actor and movie star in 30 films, and the first female film producer in India.

And that's not all. Pramila was also the winner of the very first Miss India beauty pageant – in 1947. She was 31 and pregnant with her fifth child at the time!

Esther was born to a Baghdadi Jewish family in Kolkata (called Calcutta then). At school she excelled at sports and in class. She became a kindergarten teacher but then was drawn into the world of Hindi cinema – what we know today as Bollywood. Her first job was as a dancer for a travelling theatre company that showed movies. Her job was to dance and entertain the audience for 15 minutes while the reel was changed on the projector. She was visiting her actor cousin when she was noticed by a director and the star "Pramila" was born!

Jews got involved in Bollywood through a quirk of cultural circumstances. When Indian cinema began, it was taboo for Hindu and Islamic women to appear on screen, so at first female roles were played by men, just like in Shakespeare or Monty Python. But the Jewish community in India was more liberal and Jewish women were allowed and ready to take the roles. The fact that they generally had lighter skin made them acceptable for the roles of the time.

From being the lowly entertainment between reels, Pramila burst to fame with a movie *Bhikaran*, followed by many more movies and even her own production company.

Pramila's second marriage was to a Shia Muslim, but she remained a proud and practicing Jew all her life. The children were educated in both Islam and Judaism; until today, all her descendants are connected to their Jewish roots and heritage.

Pramila may have started her entertainment life as part of the intermission, but Esther Victoria Abraham ended her life a legend – on screen and off.

Henny

Some things have to be believed to be seen.

Do you believe in miracles? Most of us say we do, but deep down, we are not quite sure.

Henny Machlis was a woman who truly believed in miracles. She believed that God ran the world. That God could do anything. She lived in a world where God controlled everything – moment to moment. The same God that split the Red Sea was the same God that would show up last minute with a delivery of barley for her hundreds of guests.

Every Shabbat, the Machlis family would fit 300 people in their tiny, Jerusalem-sized living room. Henny would prepare forty chickens, three different kugels, countless salads, four desserts, gefilte fish, chicken soup and *cholent* * – every Shabbat!

The guests – almost 150 for the Friday night meal and over 100 for the Shabbat day meal – ranged from Yeshiva bochrim to curious tourists, lonely widows and singles, to drunks and the mentally disturbed. All considered the Machlis family's love and warmth more delectable than even their ample food. Henny cooked 51 weeks a year (except for the week of Pesach) from her cramped kitchen.

Starting as newlyweds, Henny and her husband Mordechai had an open Shabbat table, which expanded gradually over the years until the overflow of guests had to be seated in the courtyard and outside the front door.

A guest once quipped, "In such an open house, why do they need a doorway anyway!?"

Hosting that number of people every week had its challenges, but nothing would deter Henny's efforts. For her, the Jewish value of hospitality – known as *hachnasat orchim* (welcoming guests) in Hebrew – was unshakeable.

Henny's philosophy was simple: Ask God for help and it will come. And it did. Every time. In so many real life stories. "In the Machlis home, miracles happened every day," one of her grandchildren once said.

Once, there was a chicken shortage in Israel, and the Machlis family faced a daunting meat-free Shabbat. No chickens? An American tourist arrived just hours before Shabbat with a surprise of 40 chickens.

Not enough time to prepare for Shabbat? No problem. 20 young men magically appeared to lend a hand. Not enough space? No sweat. The walls will shift, Henny promised. And somehow, space was made and an extra 50 people accommodated…

In the 21st century, fame is prized and fortune is coveted. But Hennie Machlis found her fame as the most openhearted person in Jerusalem and made her fortune in the *mitzvah* of welcoming guests.

This Jerusalem legend was a Shabbos Queen in our time.

*Cholent: a traditional Jewish stew prepared on a Friday and cooked overnight.

Judith

Judith Kerr
Author with a Tiger (who came to tea)
England
1923 – 2019

The famous writer CS Lewis once said about tales that "we read to know we are not alone,"

Sometimes stories, and the characters in them, can become your best friends. And friends are there through good times and bad, they are with you as you have uncomfortable thoughts or struggle with challenges.

For Judith Kerr, this was Pink Rabbit.

When Judith was nine years old, the country she lived in, Germany, became dangerous for Jews. Judith's father had been very outspoken about the Nazis, and when Hitler came to power, he fled the country. A few months later, Judith and her brother Michael were rushed by their mother, in alarming secrecy and panic, away from everything they knew – home and schoolmates and well-loved toys – never to return... They escaped by train into Switzerland and then made their way to England.

Imagine having to flee your home, your friends, everything that's familiar and loved, with just a small suitcase and one cuddly toy to give you courage and be your friend. Which toy would you choose? Your Gruffalo or your Penguin? But how can you leave Teddy behind?

Judith captured her own life story in a book called *When Hitler Stole Pink Rabbit,* which became a modern classic, read by thousands who wanted a child's eye view of the Second World War and the years leading up to the Holocaust. But for little Judith, her story wasn't just words on a page, it was how books and imaginary characters had kept her safe and happy when she had little else.

As she wrote: "In most books where children fall on hard times, they are okay because their parents can cope; the mother can cook and make beautiful clothes; the father can make furniture. Mine weren't like that."

It was stories that kept her from feeling alone.

Until the end of her life her main feeling was one of gratitude: to stress how lucky her family were to find a warm welcome in London, along with many other Jewish refugees. Even though life was hard for immigrants, in England, Judith was free to become a writer and illustrator whose books sold more than 10 million copies around the world. She created some of the best-known children's books of the 20th century, such as the *Mog* series and *The Tiger Who Came To Tea*. She was awarded an OBE (Order of the British Empire) by the Queen of England to recognise her power as one of the best storytellers of our time.

"You see a lady sitting there and she's not doing anything and you tend to forget that of course she wasn't always a little old lady. There's all this coloured stuff inside her, it's all inside, bubbling."

Judith Kerr

Claudia

Claudia Roden
British cookbook writer and cultural anthropologist
Egypt, England
1936 –

"Every recipe tells a story."

Fish and chips. Apples and honey. Shabbat and challah. All go together, right? Obviously.

Actually it depends on your history.

Unlike *challah* – the sweet plaited Shabbat bread that is generally eaten amongst the Ashkenazi communities, Shabbat breads in the Sephardic world differ from community to community. The Tunisian *bejma* is a plain, white bread shaped into a triangle that is perfectly suited for mopping up the salads typical of Sephardic meals. Ethiopian Jews prepare a yellow-tinted *dabo* for Shabbat that is cooked over an open fire in a frying pan or on a flat disc, the traditional cooking method of that region.

Claudia has spent her life collecting recipes and writing books about Jewish food, especially Egyptian and Middle Eastern Jewish food. But she collects more than just recipes – she captures the world around and behind them, the food and its eaters in places near and far.

Food is a way of keeping alive traditions and memories of a community, a family and even an individual. No doubt you have your own special family recipe from a treasured grandmother or aunt.

For Claudia, the pies stuffed with eggplant and spinach reminded her of her Turkish grandmother, while the flavourful memory of lamb with mint came from her Aleppo-born paternal grandmother. The delicious morsels captured her personal history – the Cairo of her childhood in an old Syrian Jewish merchant family, where everyone – Arabs, Greeks, Turks, Armenians, Copts and Jews – lived more or less in harmony.

When she was a schoolgirl in Paris, she and her brothers and a cousin were invited to relatives to eat *ful medames* – the purée of brown beans that is the Egyptian national dish. In Egypt, *ful* is considered poor fare but, in Paris, away from home, these rather boring beans became a way to feed homesickness, to remember Egypt's tastes, smells, way of life, and of course, its stories.

In 1956, the Jewish community was expelled from Egypt. Food, the taste of home, was the only thing most managed to bring to Europe. The rugs and the intricately carved tables were gone. But not the *dfeena*, the *kibbeh*, or the *konafa*. "People were *obsessed* by food when they came out. I didn't want us to lose them."

It was through food that she told the stories of other Jewish people – all over the world.

Claudia always includes how people in that country ate, the history of the food, the roots of the ingredients and the stories around its cooking. A recipe is history, geography, culture and food – all in one. She has won many awards for her cookbooks, but her biggest achievement is not in food, but in celebrating and preserving the stories of our people.

So the next time you take a bite of your *cholent* or *felafel*, know that you have on your lips a whole mouthful of culture.

"Every recipe tells a story."

Claudia Roden

Ashager

Ashager Araro
Israel's social media queen
Ethiopia – Israel
1991 –

Some people fight wars with weapons. Some people protest by marching on the streets. But what happens when the battle you have to fight is in people's minds, in the words they use, in the emotions they feel?

Ashager Araro chooses to combat hate and negativity on social media – and she's become so good at it, she'd been dubbed Israel's Social Media Queen.

As a black Jewish woman, Ashager has a lot to fight against. Sometimes its awful comments about people with dark skin, sometimes its nasty jibes about being a Jew or Israeli, and sometimes its low blows about being a woman.

Standing up for yourself – even if you are by yourself - doesn't bother Ashager.

Ashager was born on the roadside in 1991 as her desperate family walked from their small village to the Ethiopian capital of Addis Ababa. Because of the civil war going on in Ethiopia, Jews were no longer safe there, and so Ashager's family fled their village, hoping to be rescued by Israel. Her grandfather was killed during their escape.

Thankfully, the Israeli army was conducting Operation Solomon – an operation that airlifted hundreds of Ethiopian Jews and flying them to Israel. Ashager's family was airlifted to Israel during a daring 36-hour operation in 35 Israeli aircraft. They were among the last of the Beta Israel tribe to make it to Israel in 1991. There are around 140,000 members of the tribe living in Israel.

Known in Ethiopia as the Falasha, "the outsiders", they are thought to have been parted from the rest of the tribes of Israel for more than 2,000 years and followed Judaism as it was practised before the destruction of the First Temple in Jerusalem. Until the 19th century, they thought they were the only Jews on earth, and were surprised to meet "white" Jews! But they always dreamed of coming to the "Land of Jerusalem" – so for Ashager's family and the others, this was a dream come true.

Nevertheless, finally being in Israel was not easy. Being black in a country where most people are white means that there can be discrimination – where you're judged for the colour of your skin. On the other hand, in Ethiopia, where almost everyone is black, there Ashager faced antisemitism – she was judged for being Jewish.

It's tough always being an outsider. But Ashager understands that some of us aren't meant to belong. Some of us have to turn the world upside down and make our own place in it.

Today her Instagram handle is blackjewishmagic and she proudly defines herself as: "liberal, feminist, supports black lives and a proud Zionist."

Batya

Word-lover, avid reader, spiritual-seeker, Torah teacher, publisher-author, crazy crafter, mom of three - Batya Bricker also happens to be GM Books and Brand for Exclusive Books, the largest book chain in South Africa.

She started her working life as an architect, telling stories with bricks. Answering an advert in the newspaper, she "fell into the book-world and fell in love", so she never left. She went on to write book reviews, win awards for marketing Exclusive Books, publish 14 books, manage 4 bookfairs, add a touch of magic to PJ Library South Africa and read a gazillion bedtime stories to three boys and a dog.

To the women who raised me...

Mom, Shirley – there's good reason we are travelling this life journey together.

The Amsterdam Girls – with you cheering behind me, I feel like I can do absolutely anything.

Ilana Stein – Mind extraordinaire and friend indeed.

My sisters-in-law, Tal and Nade, I have cherished our shared lives, and Daphne, I look forward to ours.

My nieces – surrogate daughters in my world of boys.

My soul-sisters – you know who you are. Covid made that clear.

Sara Evian – who reminded me to celebrate everything I do (not all the things I didn't get to).

Penny Hochfeld – a wise woman, who touches so deeply, so gently and so authentically on books, on human relationships, on life – its sorrows and joys.

Jill van Zyl – forever my book-mama

Heather Smit – who taught me that real strength lies in doing small and ordinary with courage.

Aunty Shullie – I know and feel that you are always by my side.

Zelda Signorini – my spiritual sentinel.

The Good Life girls – the time we spent learning together has kept me going in dark times.

The Academy's Women in the Room ladies – you made me feel a part of Jewish Feminist history in the making.

Thelma Danzig – who taught me to dance and stayed in the wings to cheer me along long after the curtain fell.

Florah and Sici – your being in my life makes all the best things possible on a day to day basis.

Brene Brown, Edith Eger, Rachel Naomi Remen, without your words, I would be lost.

To the feminine in God. I am only just learning to see and celebrate You. I invite You into my life.

And to the men and boys who complete my world – brothers-in-law, nephews and most importantly, Dad, Ilan, and the incredible trio – Ezra, Dovi and Aaron – this Little Woman will always have your back.

Ilana

With degrees in Nature Conservation and English, Ilana Stein combines both in her work as a writer for conservation and ecotourism entities in southern Africa.

It is Ilana's belief that knowledge of and connection to the environment is a Jewish value, and so, with a Master's degree in Environmental Jewish Education, she lectures and writes about the relationship between Judaism and the environment. She loves to take people into nature – even through the urban jungle – to share the wonders of the natural world around us from a Jewish perspective.

Ilana lives in Joha... ...a, but gets out into the bush as ... ...ing trees and wat...

...ua Heschel:

...nning of our
...ess lies in the
u...rstanding ...at life
w...out wonde...
...li...

Mary-Anne

A plot girl from Pretoria, South Africa, Mary-Anne van der Byl is inspired by nature and our beautiful earth. Being drawn to the creative world, Mary-Anne studied graphic design after school and followed that with a degree in Environmental management. She now works for an ecotourism company where she can use her skill and combine it with her love for the environment.

She has a particular love for illustration and especially of fauna and flora around her. Hoping to share the detail and beauty of nature with the world.

It's important to spend time in nature, it cleanses the soul and allows us to reconnect with ourselves and find perspective on life.

Ronel

Ronel Pienaar is a teacher and part time designer and crafter from Pretoria.

She loves spending time in nature and with her dogs and rats and believes the closer we are to nature, the more complete we are.

She works with teenagers and has a special place for girls. She believes that every girl with a dream, becomes a woman with vision.

"every girl with a dream, becomes a woman with vision"

My heroines

Here's your chance to celebrate a few of the powerful ladies in your life, who inspire, support, love, encourage and uplift you!

Name: _____

Why she's my heroine: _____

_____

_____

Name: _____

Why she's my heroine: _____

_____

_____

Name: _____

Why she's my heroine: _____

_____

_____

My heroines

Name: _____

Why she's my heroine: _____

_____

_____

Name: _____

Why she's my heroine: _____

_____

_____

Name: _____

Why she's my heroine: _____

_____

_____

Here's your chance to celebrate yourself as a future 'Brave Jewish Girl'

My heroic qualities _____

_____

_____

_____

_____

_____

_____

What I like about myself _____

_____

_____

_____

_____

_____

_____

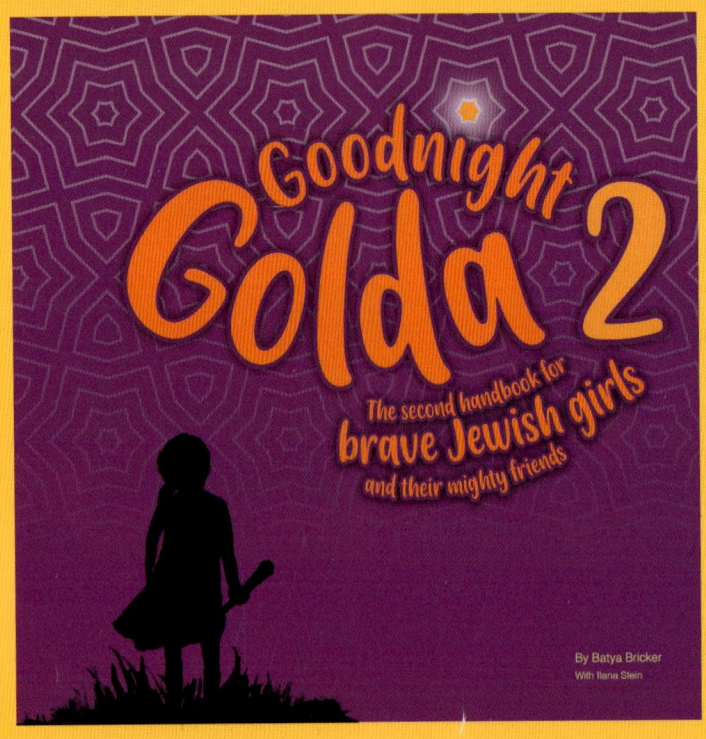

Did you love *Goodnight Golda*, but would love to see
your favourite heroine included next time?
Do you have someone to suggest for the next edition?
We are already working on *Goodnight Golda 2*!

Please send your suggestions to **www.goodnightgolda.com**, with a motivation as
to why this woman changed our world or yours.

Any other suggestions or comments are welcome - we would love to hear from you!